MY MONSTER TRUCK
GOES EVERYWHERE WITH ME

BY **KATHLEEN MARCATH**

ILLUSTRATORS: **ISAAC LIANG** AND **PARDEEP MEHRA**

MY

MONSTER

EVERYWHERE

MORNING

PURPLE

FAST

ME

HOUSE

BIG

FIRST

GO

HAPPY

PLAY

SAD

LOUD

EAT

NIGHT

NO EAT

GONE

LOOK

AFRAID

GRANDMA

PLEASE

MAYBE

THANK YOU

TIRED

SURPRISE

TRUCK

ONE

TWO

THREE

FOUR

DEDICATION

This book is dedicated with love to all children. Each of you is beautiful.
And with great joy to my precious grandchildren, whom I love and adore:

My grandson Dylan, who inspired this story.
My granddaughter Isabella, who totally believed in me.
My oldest, Dustin, the finder of things.
And the newest, precious little ones we love and adore, Ani and Ian.

To: Gertrude Johanna Ahlers Ferguson –
The promise to not let life pass me by. Xoxoxo

COPYRIGHT

Publisher's Cataloging-in-Publication data

Names: Marcath, Kathleen, author. | Liang, Isaac, illustrator. | Mehra, Pardeep, illustrator.

Title: My monster truck goes everywhere with me : illustrated in American Sign Language / by Kathleen Marcath ; illustrators: Isaac Liang and Pardeep Mehra.

Description: From verso: QR square: "Watch My Monster Truck Goes Everywhere with Me signed in American Sign Language by amazing storytellers" | Armada, MI: Kathleen Marcath, 2020 | Summary: From sunrise to sunset join Dylan with his monster truck on adventures everywhere and experience the thrill of using sign language on every page.

Identifiers: LCCN: | ISBN: 978-1-7347517-1-0 (Hardcover) | 978-1-7347517-0-3 (pbk.) | 978-1-7347517-2-7 (ebook)

Subjects: LCSH Monster trucks--Juvenile fiction. | Toys--Juvenile fiction. | Friendship--Juvenile fiction. | American Sign Language--Juvenile fiction. | CYAC Monster trucks--Fiction. | Toys--Fiction. | Friendship--Fiction. | American Sign Language--Fiction. | BISAC JUVENILE FICTION / General | JUVENILE FICTION / Family & Relationships

Classification: LCC PZ7.1.M3698 My 2020 | DDC [E]--dc23

Welcome to ASL Picture Books! We are thrilled you are holding this book in your hands! It has been a labor of love.

When you see a word typed out in all caps in **BOLD** print that is the word being signed. When you see dashes in between, it indicates the word is fingerspelled **T-R-U-C-K**.

To learn more about the production of American Sign Language or print your own ASL Alphabet chart, visit our website aslpicturebooks.com

Thank you for reading and signing along with us today! We hope you enjoy the story and learn something new.

This is **MY**

M - O - N - S - T - E - R

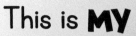

T - R - U - C - K.

is being used to represent monster truck. This is known as a *classifier*.

This is my **BIG** monster truck. He's really, really **BIG**. He's **BIG**–like a GIANT.

My BIG monster truck is **PURPLE**. He's shiny **PURPLE**– like GRAPE JELLY.

My BIG, PURPLE monster truck is **FAST**. He's **FAST**—like LIGHTNING.

My BIG, PURPLE, FAST monster truck is
LOUD. He's **LOUD**-like THUNDER.

I Love my BIG, PURPLE, FAST, **LOUD**
monster truck!

Every **MORNING** I hurry to get dressed. Then I race to the kitchen for breakfast.

My giant monster truck watches me **EAT** all my pancakes and sausages. Monster trucks don't **EAT** breakfast. I give him a hug instead.

My big monster truck goes everywhere with me. I take him along to Grandma's **HOUSE**.

Together we play all day. Grandma makes lunch for me. She signs, "**NO EAT**," and points to my monster truck." I laugh. Monster trucks can't eat lunch!

At Grandma's house my purple monster truck loves to **PLAY** monster truck games. Grandma has lots of other monster trucks for us to **PLAY** with.

FIRST, I line up all the monster trucks and have a parade. Then I build ramps. I laugh when the trucks make tracks in the mud.

Watch! My monster truck gets ready to race.
Can you count down with me?

THREE...TWO...ONE...GO!
My monster truck zooms up the ramp.

He lands with all **FOUR** wheels back on the ground.
He makes a loud, roaring engine sound.

VROOM!

My fast monster truck spins in a cloud of dust. Everyone cheers.

LOOK! My purple monster truck flipped over. A tow truck will come and tow him away. Then I will fix him with my wrench. He will be as good as new.

My monster truck goes **EVERYWHERE** with me.

At night I feel **TIRED**. Going to monster truck shows is hard work.

Mom tucks me into bed.
She says, "Good **NIGHT**."

When morning comes, I wake up, but where is my loud monster truck? He's **GONE!** I run through the house. I yell, "Monster truck, where are you?"

My big purple monster truck is lost. "Mom, help me **PLEASE!**" I have tears in my eyes. I say, "My big monster truck is gone!"

My monster truck goes everywhere with me, but where is he? I feel **SAD**. I miss my monster truck.

I feel **AFRAID**. I hope he's okay.

My mom gives me a hug.
"**MAYBE** you left your favorite
monster truck at Grandma's house."

Just then the door opens. It's
GRANDMA. She signs, "**SURPRISE!**"

Grandma smiles. She hands me my monster truck.
"Oh, **THANK YOU**, Mimi!"

I smile my biggest smile. I have my BIG, PURPLE, FAST, LOUD monster truck. He is safe. I am **HAPPY!** My monster truck will always go EVERYWHERE with me!

KATHLEEN MARCATH has a B.A. degree in Deaf Community Studies, as well as years of experience as a Special Education Sign Language Supporter has kindled her passion for helping children reach their educational potential. Kathleen is delighted to help fill the need for picture books illustrated in American Sign Language. She is a wife, mother and grandmother and resides in Michigan.

ABOUT THE ILLUSTRATORS

ISAAC LiANG ZHi JiE is a Deaf illustrator based in Singapore. At the age of four he started his artistic journey by drawing on the cupboards of his home with crayons. In his free time, he gains inspiration from traveling and café-hopping. Through his illustrations, animations, and traditional art mediums, Isaac amplifies visions and tells visual stories in a unique way.

Each page is beautifully illustrated with one or more signs sketched by Isaac Liang.

"When a Deaf child sees the illustrated pictures in this book their faces will light up."

PARDEEP MEHRA is the founder of Pencil Master Digital Studio, a family-owned business employing a large group of talented artists providing end to end illustration and publishing services.

For more than 15 years, Pardeep has been providing his keen eye, visualization and digital art skills to create hundreds of beautifully illustrated books that delight children all over the world. Pardeep lives in India with his wife Priyam and daughter Mehar. For more info and portfolio review, visit www.pencilmasterdigi.com.

Watch **MY MONSTER TRUCK GOES EVERYWHERE WITH ME** signed in American Sign Language by amazing storytellers.

Narrated by
Dennis Neubacher

CPSIA information can be obtained
at www.ICGtesting.com
Printed in the USA
LVHW071643160521
687581LV00001B/1